TOYOGRAPHY

BY SHERI TAN

HARPER FESTIVAL
An Imprint of HarperCollins Publishers

FEATURING ZURGBOT!

ZURG

PROPERTY OF

ANDY

REX

Dear Bonnie,

I am so glad the friends I had when I was growing up now have a special place in your home. They really mean a lot to me. Woody, Buzz, and the rest of the gang are the kind of pals everyone should have, and it makes me happy that you can grow up with them too.

I have to admit that it was really hard for me the day I brought you the box of my toys. I sometimes wish I was still horsing around with Woody on my shoulders or saving the world with Buzz. But when I met you, I knew that you were the right person to take care of them—someone who would play with them and give them all the love and attention they deserve.

Now that they've settled into your home, I also want you to have this special scrapbook. It's filled with photos and memories that I've kept about each of these amazing friends that you can read about with your family. You're going to have your own exciting adventures together, but I wanted you to know where they came from and what they're like! I'm sorry to miss out on the fun, but one day, I'd like to come visit and hear all about the good times you've had and all the new experiences you've had with our toys.

Take care of our friends, Bonnie. They've never let me down, and I know that they'll never let you down either.

Your pal,
Andy

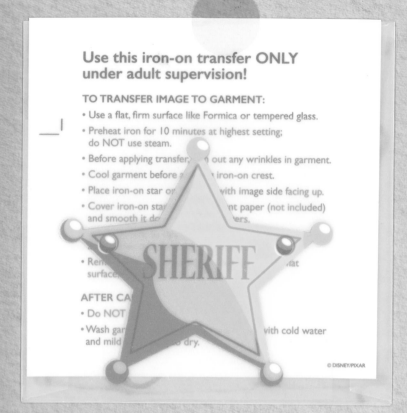

WOODY

He's brave, like a cowboy should be. He's also kind and smart. But the thing that makes Woody special is that he'll never give up on you . . . ever. He'll be your partner for life. Woody has been my pal for as long as I can remember. He was given to me when I was little, and I can't tell you how excited I was. I must have pulled that string to hear him talk a zillion times! He was my favorite toy, not just because he's a friend that I could have epic adventures with, but also because he's the kind of person I always wanted to be: He's smart and loyal, and he always knows what to do. Of course I had a cowboy hat just like his, too!

Honestly, I love Woody so much I was going to take him to college with me, but somehow he ended up in the same box as the other toys. I don't know how, but when you saw him in the box, you instantly seemed to know him. Something told me that he could be your best friend, just like he was mine. I hope that you're playing with him every day and having just as much fun with him as I did. It was really tough to let Woody go, but I'm happy he's with you now, along with the rest of the gang.

BUZZ LIGHTYEAR

Buzz Lightyear is just about the coolest toy ever! He's sworn to protect the galaxy from the Evil Emperor Zurg, and he can shoot lasers! And he can fly! Like Woody, he's loyal and you can always depend on him to keep his word and get the job done. He's the law enforcement of the future. With Buzz, it's like a whole new world opened up and anything is possible. Like he says, "To infinity and beyond!"

Buzz is a space ranger from the Intergalactic Alliance, stationed in the Gamma Quadrant of Sector 4. My mom gave him to me for my seventh birthday. He has a helmet that he flips open when he knows that the air around him is safe to breathe. His space suit keeps him safe when he travels in space. It has everything, like a control panel with three buttons on the right side of his chest. One lets him communicate with Star Command,

BUZZ LIGHTYEAR TO THE RESCUE!

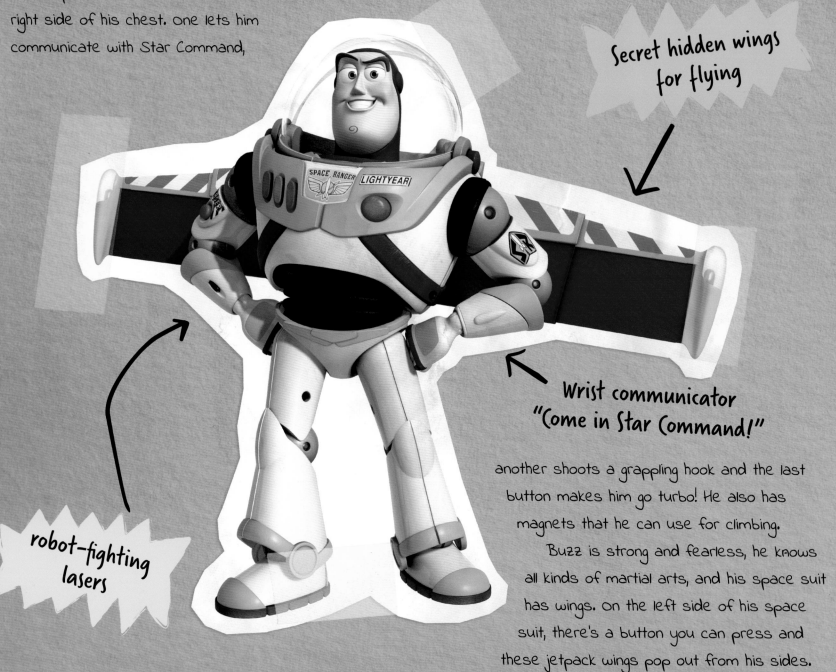

Secret hidden wings for flying

robot-fighting lasers

Wrist communicator "Come in Star Command!"

another shoots a grappling hook and the last button makes him go turbo! He also has magnets that he can use for climbing.

Buzz is strong and fearless, he knows all kinds of martial arts, and his space suit has wings. On the left side of his space suit, there's a button you can press and these jetpack wings pop out from his sides.

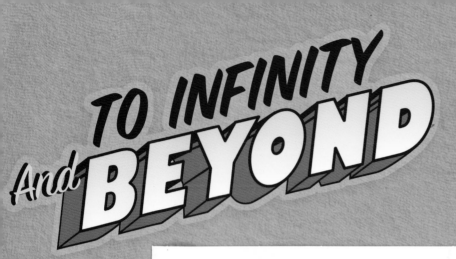

TO INFINITY And BEYOND

Not today, Zurg!

INSTRUCTION MANUAL

SPACE RANGER

AL INFINITO Y MÁS ALLÁ

BEST FRIENDS

When people ask me who my best friend was growing up, I always say Sheriff Woody. He was always there for me, no matter what. We used to have so many adventures together. I took him with me everywhere I went—except the time I had to leave him home when I went to cowboy camp because his arm was ripped. Cowboy camp was not the same without him.

Then I got Buzz Lightyear for my birthday, and he became my best buddy too. I wrote my name on his boot, just like I did with Woody. I would always try to take him along, except when Mom said I could only take one toy. I liked to imagine that he and Woody were best friends, and that they'd do anything for each other.

There was one time when we went to the beach and I took both of them along. When we were packing up to leave at the end of the day, I had Buzz with me, but I couldn't find Woody. I started to panic, and Mom had to tell me to calm down. Mom, Molly, and I looked all over, and we couldn't find him. But I wasn't going home without Woody.

Just as Mom was about to give up because it was getting really late, I dropped Buzz on the sand by accident. When I picked him up, I saw a cowboy boot sticking out of the sand. It was Woody! I was so happy I started jumping up and down and hollering. It was like Buzz found Woody. That's what best friends do. They never give up on each other, and that's why I think Buzz and Woody are partners for life.

 WOODY WAS THE FIRST EXTRATERRESTRIAL I MET WHEN I CRASH-LANDED ON ANDY'S BED.

 Buzz thought he was a real space ranger!

I HAD TO PUT THINGS IN ORDER ON THIS UNTAMED TERRAIN. THE LOCALS DIDN'T HAVE A REAL LEADER.

We were just fine before you came along. I had things in order.

EVEN THOUGH I WASN'T IMPRESSED WITH SHERIFF WOODY AT FIRST, IT TURNS OUT HE IS THE BEST PARTNER ANYONE COULD HAVE. HE RESCUED ME EVEN WHEN HE DIDN'T HAVE TO.

Well, actually, I did have to . . .

THE SHERIFF AND I HAVE BEEN THROUGH A LOT TOGETHER: CHASING CARS AND JETLINERS, ESCAPING ROCKET BLASTS AND INCINERATORS. AND ALL BECAUSE HE TAUGHT ME THAT WHAT MATTERS IS TO BE LOVED BY A KID. AND TO ALWAYS BE THERE FOR THEM.

 I couldn't believe my eyes when I saw Buzz. Sure, he looked awesome with that shiny white space suit, but he was in MY spot on Andy's bed! And then everyone fell for him and his fancy gadgets.

 I CAN'T HELP BEING CHARMING.

Then things went from bad to worse, and I ended up in the toy chest instead of on Andy's bed. I had to do something.

YEAH, YOU DID SOMETHING ALL RIGHT. YOU THREW ME OUT THE WINDOW!

It was an accident! But no one believed me, so I had to go rescue Buzz on my own. I was trying to get us both back home to Andy, but we ended up in the home of the meanest kid on the block—Sid!

THAT WAS WHEN I FOUND OUT THAT I REALLY WAS A TOY, AND THAT ALL MY BUTTONS AND LASERS WERE JUST FOR PLAY.

But Buzz got us to Andy, even with an explosive rocket strapped to his back.

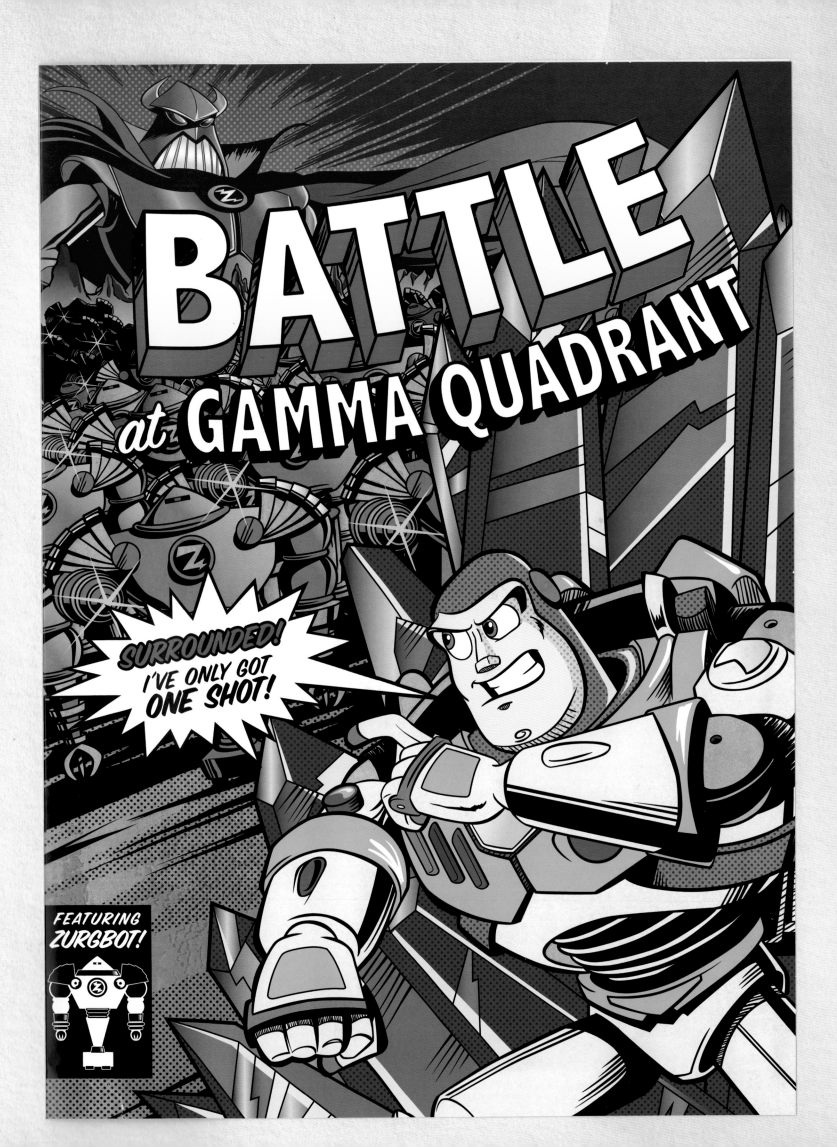

MY OTHER FRIENDS

REX

Roar!

Rex is the meanest, most terrifying dinosaur who ever lived! He's a *Tyrannosaurus rex*. Look at his big teeth. But you know, even though he might seem scary, he's really a big softie. He just wants you to hug him and play with him. Truth is, he's actually a little timid.

And don't worry that he has short arms. Rex has a really awesome tail that can be used to take down powerful villains.

I kind of wish I had gotten him a dinosaur buddy, but now he has Trixie, your special *Triceratops*. Together, I know they are going to be a super dinosaur team!

HAMM

Hamm is a pink piggy bank that will keep your money safe—most of the time. (Sometimes coins can fall out of the slot at the top.) Just make sure you keep the cork in his belly in place and stand him on his four legs. Hamm is a funny guy who likes to tell jokes. He'll tell you his favorite karate move is the pork chop or that when pigs put a blanket on the ground, it's a pig-nic. Something tells me that he's kind of a know-it-all who likes to tell the other toys what he thinks.

BO PEEP

Even though she's not with all the toys I gave you, I want to mention a special toy that had a lot of great adventures with all the friends you have now. Bo Peep is a shepherdess with three sheep. She's actually made of porcelain and was part of my sister Molly's lamp, but Molly let me include her in all the fun. Woody was Bo Peep's hero and he always came to her rescue. I'm not sure where she is now, but who knows? She just might show up again one day!

MR. POTATO HEAD AND MRS. POTATO HEAD

No matter what you do, you've got to keep Mr. and Mrs. Potato Head together. They're madly in love. I got Mrs. Potato Head—well, actually, my sister Molly did—the first Christmas in our new house, and I just know that Mr. Potato Head was super happy when she moved in. They were just meant to be together and will do anything to help each other out.

As I'm sure you've found out, Mr. and Mrs. Potato Head can separate their body parts from their potato bodies and switch them around. Sometimes when I've been in a hurry to clean up after playing with them, I've stuck the body parts in the wrong places, and they end up looking like weird modern art.

Mr. Potato Head can be grumpy at times—and a little rude. He even has angry eyes for when he's mad. But he'll always lend a hand if you really need help, and Mrs. Potato Head always knows how to calm her husband down. She adores Mr. Potato Head and will also lend him a hand, an eye, or any other body part if he needs it. Most of the time she's a sweet lady, but trust me, she has a temper too.

SLINKY DOG

Slinky is like the toy version of my dog, Buster. When Buster was a pup, he was really playful, just like Slinky. And Slinky is as loyal a dog as you could ever want, just like Buster.

Slinky is Woody's best dog friend. He'll do anything for Sheriff Wood  floppy ears, and when you he'll come running, with his tongue hanging out. Slinky's head, legs, and rear end are plastic, but his body is all spring, which comes in handy when you need him to stretch really far to rescue someone or grab anything.

PIZZA PLANET

Pizza Planet is the coolest restaurant. It's got my two favorite things in one awesome place: pizza and games! Mom took Molly and me there whenever we got good grades in school, if she thought Molly and I deserved a reward, or when she just didn't feel like cooking. The restaurant looks like Saturn on the outside, with a big ring around it. There are two robot guards at the entrance, both holding shields that look like pizzas and long spears with pepperoni slices at the tips. It's awesome. "You are clear to enter. Welcome to Pizza Planet!" they say before the doors slide open. It feels like you're entering a spaceship. Also, there is a huge red and white rocket outside.

Pizza Planet has all kinds of games, like ring toss, Hit the Clown, and whack-a-Alien, plus rocket ship rides and lots of arcade machines. And of course they have pizza, lots of different kinds of pizza, but they also serve Supernova Burgers and drinks called Alien Slime that shoot out of dispensers that look like venus flytraps. In the middle of the restaurant, there's a rocket ship crane game. It has a claw you can use to try to pull out a squeaky green Alien toy.

THE ALIENS

This little green Alien with three eyes is the toy that you can pull out of the crane game at Pizza Planet. I can't tell you how many times I played that game over the years and never managed to grab any of those toys. I still don't know how I ended up with three of them in my house.

Kids Menu

Entrées

SOLAR ECLIPSE (MINI CHEESE PIZZA)

MOON PIE (MINI PEPPERONI PIZZA)

ASTEROID BELT (SPAGHETTI WITH MEATBALLS)

SUPERNOVA BURGER

SPACE CHICKEN (CHICKEN FINGERS)

MAC & GREEN CHEESE*

Sweet Treats

COSMIC COOKIE SANDWICH

BLASTOFF BROWNIE SUNDAE

BIG DIPPER ICE CREAM BOWL

Drinks

MILK

SODA

ALIEN SLIME

Milky Way Shakes

CHOCOLATE

VANILLA

STRAWBERRY

*Our signature Mac & Green Cheese is blended with all natural ingredients and 100% safe to eat.

AL'S TOY BARN

I loved going to Al's Toy Barn in my old neighborhood. I used to laugh at the TV commercial with Al in his chicken suit laying an egg, telling all the kids to go to his store, where everything there was "cheep, cheep, cheep!" You could tell you were at Al's 'cause there was a big chicken out front by the road, just before you turned into the parking lot. The store had all kinds of toys and bikes, skateboards, video games, books, remote-control cars . . . you name it, they had it! It was a wonderland of toys.

Molly and I would tell Mom which toys we wanted for Christmas and for our birthdays. She always said that our lists of toys were too long. I didn't think there could ever be a list that was too long! Sometimes at Christmas, she would take us there to meet Santa Claus, who would give out candy canes to all the kids who took a picture with him.

Anyway, Al's Toy Barn was huge, with rows and rows of toys. It was like a supermarket, but much better, because it had toys. When I walked through the sliding glass doors of the store, I wouldn't know what I wanted to see first: the bubble-making guns or the cowboy toys or the construction sets or the dinosaurs or superheroes or space toys or . . . There were just too many things—and I wanted it all.

Mom always took Molly to look at the dolls and tea sets. Sometimes I would tag along with them just to keep them company, but most of the time I went straight to the cowboy stuff. But then the space

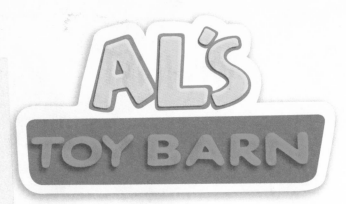

toys came along and then I would stare at the Buzz Lightyear toys for hours. When Mom surprised me by getting Buzz for me on my seventh birthday, that was insanely awesome!

Al's Toy Barn also had a section for old toys. They called them vintage toys. When I say old, I mean these toys were made way before I was born. Al kept them in special glass display cases in a small room in the back of the store. Kids could only go in there with a grown-up, and all the toys back there were at least a hundred dollars or more. Mom thought it was crazy to pay that much money for a toy, but I liked to see what people used to play with.

JESSIE

Jessie is the roughest, toughest cowgirl in the whole west. Before I found out what her name was, I called her Bazooka Jane. I think that kind of suited her 'cause she's brave and she's always up for an adventure. She also loves all kinds of critters, but none more than her old pal Bullseye. What's extra cool about Jessie is that she can yodel. She yodels to call animals for help. She's also great at using the lasso. Whenever you need someone to round up the bad guys, just call Jessie! She and Woody—and Bullseye too, of course—make a great team. And Jessie will surely be there whenever you need a hand or some company. No one can ever feel sad when Jessie's around!

Yee-haw!

Yo-de-lay-hee-hoo!

There's nothing like a good adventure!

Way to go, cowpoke!

BULLSEYE

Bullseye is Woody's horse, and he'll do anything for Woody. He's a lovable horse who can ride like the wind and even leap across canyons. He's always happy and likes to do things to make other people happy. I think he's just like an overgrown puppy dog. Jessie loves Bullseye and is always giving him extra hugs.

WOODY'S TV SHOW

SHERIFF WOODY NO LONGER IN CHARGE

POPULAR CHILDREN'S TV SHOW CANCELED

After just one season, the once-beloved Saturday morning children's show *Woody's Roundup* has been put out to pasture. Sheriff Woody, the rootinest, tootinest cowboy of the Wild West, has hung up his hat after a cliffhanger that we may never see resolved.

Using puppets and lively music, the show featured a dashing and good-natured hero, Sheriff Woody Pride, who never once failed to outsmart the bad guys and bring justice to the land. Sheriff Woody was always with his trusty steed, Bullseye, and an enthusiastic cowgirl named Jessie who would yodel to call creatures for help. There was also a wise and friendly prospector, Stinky Pete, who often gave advice and was sometimes the butt of jokes—like when a pickax got stuck in his, uh, behind. *Woody's Roundup* was a wholesome, cheerful program that children and parents enjoyed together.

The cancelation came as a shock, since the last-aired episode showed Jessie and the Prospector trapped in an abandoned gold mine. The Prospector had mistakenly lit a stick of dynamite, thinking it was a candle, and it was about to blow. In the meantime, Jessie yodeled for her critter friends to get Sheriff Woody. He and Bullseye came bounding up through the Grand Canyon to save the day, but just as they leaped off a cliff to get to the other side of the ravine, the show announcer cut in to say, "Tune in next time for 'Woody's Finest Hour!'" Only later did audiences learn they'd have to use their imaginations to figure out what happened next.

The immense popularity of the show led to a whole roundup of merchandise, including toys, hats, posters, cookie jars, money banks, games, record players, yo-yos, clothes . . . the list goes on and on. No doubt these will soon turn up in yard sales everywhere.

"Times have changed," the show's producers explained. "Space is the new frontier, and children are now more interested in astronauts, rocket ships, and space aliens that battle each other." Unfortunately, this means that unless Sheriff Woody one day becomes a space cowboy, he no longer has a place in TV land. It will be interesting to see where this new interest in all things space will take us: space rangers traveling the universe in fancy rocket ships battling Martians or Saturnians or aliens from another galaxy? We will have to wait and see. In the meantime, so long, Sheriff Woody. Happy trails to you and the rest of the Roundup Gang.

A COWBOY & SPACE RANGER ADVENTURE

woo woo!

As the train roars through the canyon—*clickety-clack, clickety-clack*—the roof of a train car explodes and One-Eyed Bart bursts out. Bart tosses a bag of money onto the roof. His one eye gleams as he proudly holds up two more bags cackling, "Ha ha ha ha! Money, money, money!"

Suddenly, a lasso whips the moneybag out of his hand. "Hey!" One-Eyed Bart yells as he falls backward. Bart tries to get up, but he can't—not with Sheriff Woody pinning him down. "You got a date with justice, One-Eyed Bart!" Woody declares, staring angrily down at the thief.

Bart tries to get up, only to find the sheriff's boot on his face. "Too bad, Sheriff, I'm a married man," he says smugly.

With a loud cry of "Haiya!" One-Eyed Bart's wife, One-Eyed Betty, flips onto the roof of the train. Betty marches toward Sheriff Woody, who backflips all the way to the back of the train. "Whoa," he says, as he steadies himself on the edge of the roof.

Betty casts an evil look at the sheriff—before whacking him with her red purse. Woody has been knocked off the train! Betty turns to her husband, who is now right by her side, holding up a remote control with a big red button. He presses it and the bridge up ahead blows up! *oh no!*

Woody and Jessie hop on Bullseye and take off, as Woody yells out, "The orphans!" The train is loaded with children on their way to the local orphanage.

Just then—*screech!*—three Aliens come driving up in a pink convertible. One-Eyed Bart and Betty hop off the train roof and onto the car. Woody can't stop the villains *and* save the orphans.

Bullseye rides like the wind and soon catches the train. "Hold 'em steady!" Woody tells Jessie, as he leaps onto the locomotive. Quickly, he pulls on the brake but the train doesn't stop in time. It goes over the edge of the tracks, falling down, down, down into a canyon. There is a second of silence, and then, *boom!*

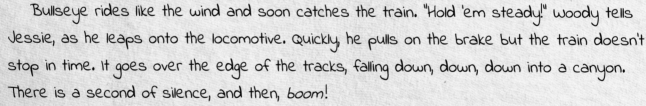

Jessie and Bullseye hang their heads in sorrow. They tried their best, but now they've lost the train, the orphans, and their hero. But by golly, the train rises out of the canyon! Who's come to the rescue?

It's Buzz Lightyear! "Glad I could catch the train!" he says, holding it up above him.

"Now let's go catch some criminals," Woody says, waving safely from inside the train.

Buzz puts the train down on the ground and takes to the skies once again. He aims his laser at One-Eyed Bart's getaway car and shoots it, splitting the car in two!

SUNNYSIDE

Sunnyside Daycare seems like a really fun place, Bonnie. I bet you have fun there every day, especially because your mom works there too. I've been to Sunnyside a few times. I'd go with my mom to donate toys that Molly and I no longer played with. It looks like a really cheerful place. I wish I were a lot younger so I could go there too! Maybe not the Caterpillar Room, because that seems a little hectic with the smaller kids. But the Butterfly Room, where you go to class, looks like it would be loads of fun. It must have been nice to play in the playground outside on sunny days.

I didn't get to see many of the toys in the Butterfly Room, but I think I saw a very huggable pink bear. Molly would have loved him when she was your age.

Bonnie,

I drew a picture of the bear I saw at Sunnyside while I was
there waiting for my mom one day. I thought you might like it.
He seems like a happy bear.

Andy

NEW FRIENDS

I loved meeting your toys, Bonnie. I couldn't be happier to see that Woody and Buzz's family of friends has grown to include your friends too.

TRIXIE

Rex is going to have awesome adventures with Trixie. I imagine she's funny and friendly, and I know Rex always wanted to have a dinosaur partner. A *T. rex* and a *Triceratops* make a super dinosaur team!

PEAS-IN-A-POD

Those plushy green peas are adorable in the zipper pouch that makes up their pod.

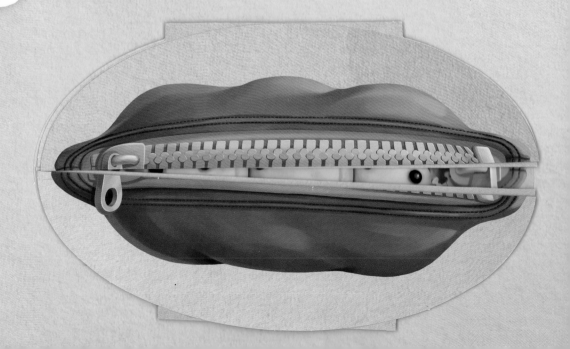

DOLLY

I bet you enjoy playing dress-up with Dolly. I know my sister Molly would have loved having a pretty rag doll like Dolly when she was younger. I love her purple hair and googly eyes. I hear that you can make different outfits for her. That sounds awesome!

MR. PRICKLEPANTS

Mr. Pricklepants is the coolest hedgehog I have ever met. He looks dashing in his green lederhosen and green hat with the orange feather. Even though he's supposed to be prickly, he is actually quite fuzzy and cuddly.

BUTTERCUP

Buttercup is a special unicorn. You just look into his blue eyes, and you know there's something magical about him. Something tells me that he also likes to tell jokes, so he's probably going to get along really well with Hamm.

CHUCKLES THE CLOWN

Even though Chuckles has a sad smile, I think that, deep down, he is a happy clown. He must be happy to be in a home where he gets played with all the time.

GROWING UP

When I was your age, Bonnie, I didn't think about growing up and living away from my family. But here I am, in college and far away from the things and the people I grew up with. I miss my mom and my sister, Molly, and just being with them. They say the people you grow up with and the things that you've been through help make you who you are today. I think that's really true.

Mom has always been there for me. I don't know how she did it; she always had time for me even after Molly was born, though she was still busy with work. She would be there when I was sick, or that time I scraped my knees and elbows pretty good when I fell off my bike. She was always there to cheer me on at soccer games. Somehow, she made every birthday and Christmas the best ones ever. She was the kind of mom that my friends even liked hanging out with.

I didn't think much about it before, but now I realize that one of the most important things she taught me was to make my own decisions. It could have been about which toy to take with me to Pizza Planet, or what I should do with the stuff in my room . . . simple stuff like that. But those little choices helped me get used to deciding what to do on my own. She never made me wonder if I made the right call.

When Molly came along, I was excited! I was also thinking that it was a good thing she was a girl, 'cause I thought that meant that she would have her own toys to play with and wouldn't touch mine. But we shared a room when we lived in my first house, so there was no getting around that. Once, I found Mr. Potato Head covered in drool in her crib. I can't imagine he was too happy about that. But I let her play with Hamm and

Buzz and everyone. I included her in some of our adventures too. She was the 50-foot baby on a rampage! Molly also let me play with Bo Peep and her sheep, which were actually part of her lamp.

Molly's almost a teenager now, but she will always be my baby sister. She'd prefer to read magazines and hang out with her school friends than play with her toy friends, but I know she still has a picture of her and Barbie. Once in a while, she'll say something to me like, "Remember when we had a race to see who could go down the stairs faster, me or Slinky Dog?" or "Remember when I tried to find out how much stuff I could put in Hamm till his cork popped out?"

That's when I know she misses our old friends too.

Before I gave you the toys, I was going to store them up in the attic. Well, except for Woody. He was going to go to college with me. But a note on the box I was going to store them in had your address on it. So I brought the toys to your house. I'd never met you or seen your place before, but when I saw you playing with your toys in the garden, I had a very good feeling about you. It reminded me of how I played with my toys when I was younger.

I saw how your eyes lit up as I took out each toy: Jessie, Bullseye, Rex, Mr. and Mrs. Potato Head, Slinky Dog, Hamm, the Aliens, and Buzz Lightyear. And you looked in the box for another toy and said, "My cowboy!" It was like you knew him.

When you reached for Woody, I have to admit that I wasn't sure whether I was going to give him to you. But when I asked, "You think you can take care of him for me?" you nodded your head and gave Woody the biggest hug ever. That's when I knew for sure that Woody—and all his friends—would always be happy with you.

Bonnie,

I hope you will treasure this collection of memories for a long time. My toys were pretty special to me. Thank you for sharing your home and your heart with them. I know Woody, Buzz, Jessie, and the rest of the gang will love going on adventures with you and that you will never feel lonely when they're around. They'll be your anchor when everything else around you changes. They will listen when you need someone to talk to, and they will be there whenever you need a hug. The toys will show you that friends come in all shapes and sizes and that there's no limit to the kinds of adventures you will have—and I'm sure you'll have plenty. These toys are the best, and I hope you have as much fun with them as I did. As a good friend of ours says: To infinity and beyond!

So long, partner.

Your pal,
Andy

P.S. Have fun with the stickers. Now you can make this scrapbook your own!

HARPER FESTIVAL

An Imprint of HarperCollinsPublishers

For information address HarperCollins Children's Books,
a division of HarperCollins Publishers, 195 Broadway,
New York, NY 10007.
www.harpercollins.com

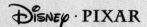
Produced by

INSIGHT KIDS

An Imprint of Insight Editions
PO Box 3088
San Rafael, CA 94912
www.insighteditions.com

Publisher: Raoul Goff

Associate Publisher: Vanessa Lopez

Creative Director: Chrissy Kwasnik

Senior Designer: Stuart Smith

Senior Editor: Paul Ruditis

Production Editor: Lauren LePera

Senior Production Manager: Greg Steffen

Insight Editions would like to thank Samantha Johnson and Kaia
Waller for their editorial assistance, and Lucio De Giuseppe and Julya
Pinchuck for providing additional artwork.

Manufactured in China by Insight Editions

18 19 20 21 22 CJ 10 9 8 7 6 5 4 3 2 1